WHAT KiND of CAR DOES a T. REX DRiVE?

MARK LEE
BRiAN BiGGS

putnam

G. P. PUTNAM'S SONS

Uncle Otto was having a summer sale.

But so far, no one had come to buy his cars.

"Where are all the customers?" Ava asked.

"Maybe they're all on vacation," Mickey said.

"Well, I'm not on vacation!" Otto said.

"I will sell a car to anyone—or anything—that shows up!"

And that's when a **Stegosaurus** lumbered onto the lot.
"I'm looking for a car," he said. "What do you recommend?"
Uncle Otto had never sold a car to a dinosaur.
He didn't know what to say.

"Don't worry, Uncle Otto," Ava said.
"He's a plant eater."
"Okay," Otto replied. "But what kind of car does he want?"

"What about an off-road vehicle?" Mickey asked the dinosaur. "You can drive deep into the forest to find mosses and ferns to snack on."

LOW
PRICES

"Perfect!" the Stegosaurus said.
He jumped into the car, honked the horn,
and drove away.

"Uncle Otto! Look!"

But just then, a **Pterodactyl** glided down from the sky.

"Not now, Mickey," Otto said. "I want to sell a car to a . . ."

"A Pterodactyl," Ava whispered.

"It's too hot to fly," the Pterodactyl said. "Maybe I need to buy a car."

"You like the wind, and you're a fish eater,"
Mickey said. "How about a convertible?
You can drive to the beach and glide
from the cliffs to the ocean."

"Good idea!" the Pterodactyl said.
He hopped into his new car
and headed for the shore.

"Uncle Otto! You'd better take a look at this!"

But just then, a **Triceratops** ambled into view.

"Not now, Mickey," Uncle Otto said. "I'm busy selling a car to a . . ."

"A Triceratops," Ava said.

"Great horns," Otto told the dinosaur.
"I bet you win a lot of arguments."

"I'm a gentle giant," the Triceratops said.
"Do you have a vehicle that might suit me?"

HOT
BUY

"What about a delivery van?" Mickey suggested.
"The back is empty, and you can get in through
the rear doors."

"You're a dear," the Triceratops said.
She climbed into the van and waved
as she drove away.

"Um . . . Uncle Otto . . . ?"
"What's the problem, Mickey?"

Suddenly, there was a loud *thump-thump-thump*, and a **Tyrannosaurus Rex** appeared.

"The Stegosaurus and the Pterodactyl and the Triceratops bought cars," the T. Rex said. "I want to buy a car, too!"

"Certainly! How about this nice microcar?" Uncle Otto suggested. "You can park it anywhere."

HUGE DEAL

"I could never fit inside that!" the T. Rex bellowed. Then he squashed the microcar with his powerful legs.

"I hear you loud and clear, Mr. Rex. What about this family minivan?"

The T. Rex bared his razor-sharp teeth. "Can you really see me driving a minivan?"

"A taxicab?"

"I'm not taking anyone for a ride!"

"A sport-utility vehicle?"

"I don't like sports!"

Uncle Otto was starting to sweat.
"HELP!" he squeaked at Mickey and Ava.
The children whispered back and forth.
Finally, they turned to the T. Rex.

DRIVE IT HOME

"Follow us.
We know the
perfect car
for you."

"A MONSTER TRUCK!"

The T. Rex *loved* the humongous wheels.
He let out a roar of delight and hit the road.

"I'm changing the name of the
business," Uncle Otto said.
"Dinosaurs are great customers."
    "Maybe you should hire us
to help out," Ava said.
    "That won't be necessary.
I'm a dinosaur expert!"

OTTO'S
DINO CARS

That's when a REALLY big customer stepped onto the lot.

THE END

For my grandson—M.L.   For my dad—B.B.

G. P. PUTNAM'S SONS
an imprint of Penguin Random House LLC, New York

Text copyright © 2019 by Mark Lee.
Illustrations copyright © 2019 by Brian Biggs.

G. P. Putnam's Sons is a registered trademark of Penguin Random House LLC.

Visit us online at penguinrandomhouse.com

Library of Congress Cataloging-in-Publication Data
Names: Lee, Mark, 1950– author. | Biggs, Brian, illustrator.
Title: What kind of car does a T. Rex drive? / Mark Lee ; illustrated by Brian Biggs.
Description: New York, NY : G. P. Putnam's Sons, [2019]
Summary: Uncle Otto is a used car salesman who, with the help of his
niece and nephew, finds the perfect vehicles for his dinosaur customers.
Identifiers: LCCN 2017012119 | ISBN 9781524741235 (hc) |
ISBN 9781524741242 (epub fixed) | ISBN 9781524741266 (kf8/kindle)
Subjects: | CYAC: Dinosaurs—Fiction. | Automobiles—Fiction.
Classification: LCC PZ7.L51394 Wh 2019 | DDC [E]—dc23
LC record available at https://lccn.loc.gov/2017012119

Manufactured in China by RR Donnelley Asia Printing Solutions Ltd.
ISBN 9781524741235
1 3 5 7 9 10 8 6 4 2

Design by Dave Kopka. Text set in Neutraface Text.
The art was drawn in brush and ink and colored digitally in Photoshop.